WEE LITTLE
BUNNY

By Lauren Thompson
Illustrated by John Butler

Simon & Schuster Books for Young Readers
New York   London   Toronto   Sydney

It was spring in the meadow
and the wee little bunny
was all brand-new.

This wee little bunny
was a busy little bunny.

"What will you do today?"
asked his sweet Mama dear.

"Everything!" said the bunny,
and—*run, run, run!*—
he chased a dragonfly.

"Let's hide inside this log!"
said the stripy chipmunk brown.

"Chase me first!" called the bunny,
and—*giggle, giggle, giggle!*—
he dashed through the grass.

"Settle down, now!"
grumped the prickly porcupine.

"Sorry, sir!" said the bunny,
and—*tippy-tippy-toe!*—
he splashed across the brook.

"Time to hop on home!"
sang the chickadee-dee-dee.

"Soon!" called the bunny, and—*wiggle, wiggle, wiggle!*— he tumbled in the clover.

Then the wee bunny heard
Mama call, "Story time!"
and he scampered—*fast, fast, fast!*—
right to Mama's side.

"There's my busy, dizzy bunny!"
said Mama with a tickle.
"Won't you sit a little while
and tell your busy tale?"

"Oh, yes!" said the bunny.
Then—*snuggle, snuggle, snuggle!*—
he told the happy tale of
his busy, dizzy day!

To Nina, my newest niece.—L. T.
To Oliver Thomas—J. B.

SIMON & SCHUSTER BOOKS FOR YOUNG READERS
An imprint of Simon & Schuster Children's Publishing Division
1230 Avenue of the Americas, New York, New York 10020
Text copyright © 2010 by Lauren Thompson
Illustrations copyright © 2010 by John Butler
All rights reserved, including the right of reproduction in whole or in part in any form.
SIMON & SCHUSTER BOOKS FOR YOUNG READERS is a trademark of Simon & Schuster, Inc.
For information about special discounts for bulk purchases, please contact Simon & Schuster
Special Sales at 1-866-506-1949 or business@simonandschuster.com.
The Simon & Schuster Speakers Bureau can bring authors to your live event. For more information or to book an event,
contact the Simon & Schuster Speakers Bureau at 1-866-248-3049 or visit our website at www.simonspeakers.com.
Book design by Tom Daly
The text for this book is set in Neutra Text.
The illustrations for this book are rendered in acrylic paint and colored pencils.
Manufactured in China
2 4 6 8 10 9 7 5 3 1
Library of Congress Cataloging-in-Publication Data
Thompson, Lauren.
Wee little bunny / Lauren Thompson;
illustrated by John Butler.—
1st ed.
p. cm.—(Wee little ; #3)
Summary: A young rabbit enjoys a "busy, dizzy" day of playing in the meadow near his home.
ISBN: 978-1-4424-0210-2
[1. Rabbits—Fiction. 2. Meadow animals—Fiction. 3. Animals—Infancy—Fiction.] I. Butler, John, 1952- ill. II. Title.
PZ7.T37163Web 2009
[E]—dc22
2008044911